T0192915

MATT PHELAN

PIGNIC

GREENWILLOW BOOKS, *An Imprint of* HarperCollins*Publishers*

Pignic. Copyright © 2018 by Matt Phelan. All rights reserved. Manufactured in China. For information address HarperCollins Children's Books, a division of HarperCollins Publishers, 195 Broadway, New York, NY 10007. www.harpercollinschildrens.com. Watercolors and pencils were used to prepare the full-color art. The text type is Adobe Caslon Pro.

Library of Congress Cataloging-in-Publication Data
Names: Phelan, Matt, author, illustrator.
Title: Pignic / written and illustrated by Matt Phelan.
Description: First edition. | New York, NY : Greenwillow Books, an imprint of HarperCollinsPublishers, [2018] | Summary: "A pig experiences adversity but in the end enjoys a perfect summer day"—Provided by publisher.
Identifiers: LCCN 2016050279 | ISBN 9780062443397 (hardcover)
Subjects: | CYAC: Pigs—Fiction. | Play—Fiction. | Summer—Fiction.
Classification: LCC PZ7.P44882 Pi 2018 | DDC [E]—dc23 LC record available at https://lccn.loc.gov/2016050279
22 SCP 10 9 8 7 6 5
First Edition

Greenwillow Books

For Jasper

It's a perfect day for a pignic.

There is a tree to climb!

Uh-oh.

Too high.

HOORAY!

There is a kite to fly!

Uh-oh.

No wind.

HUFF
PUFF

HOORAY!

Pretzels! Pies! Pickles!
And plums!

Uh-oh.

Dark clouds.

Mud?

Mud!

HOORAY!

HOORAY!

What a perfect day for a pignic.